Western Pony

Do you love ponies? Be a Pony Pal!

Look for these Pony Pal books:

Pony Pals

Western Pony

Jeanne Betancourt

illustrated by Vivien Kubbos

SCHOLASTIC INC.
New York Toronto London Auckland Sydney
Mexico City New Delhi Hong Kong

No part of this publication may be reproduced in whole or in part, or stored in a retrieval system, or transmitted in any form or by any means, electronic, mechanical, photocopying, recording, or otherwise, without written permission of the publisher. For information regarding permission, write to Scholastic Australia Pty Limited ACN 000 614 577, PO Box 579, Gosford 2250.

ISBN 0-439-06488-0

Text copyright © 1999 by Jeanne Betancourt. Cover and text illustrations copyright © 1999 by Scholastic Australia. All rights reserved. Published by Scholastic Inc., 555 Broadway, New York, NY 10012, by arrangement with Scholastic Australia Pty Limited. PONY PALS, SCHOLASTIC and associated logos are trademarks and/or registered trademarks of Scholastic Inc.

12 11 10 9 8 7 (2 3 4/0

Printed in the U.S.A.   40

First Scholastic printing, September 1999
Cover and text illustrations by Vivien Kubbos
Typeset in Bookman

For Susan and Jeff

A special thanks to Margaret Barney of Broken Wheel Ranch.

Contents

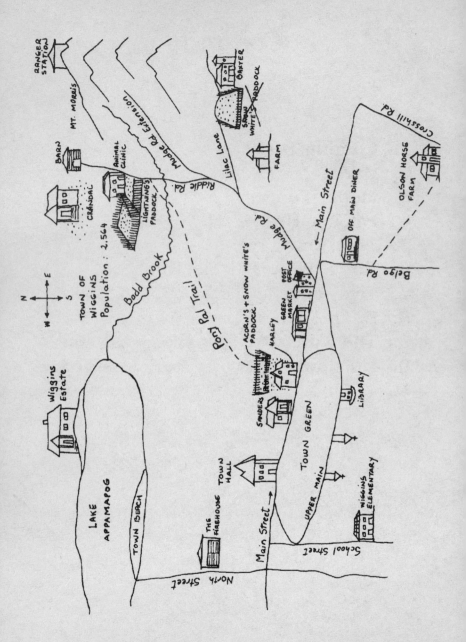

Coming Home

Lulu Sanders and her father drove into Wiggins after a two-week vacation. "I'm glad to be home," Lulu said as they turned onto Main Street. "I missed Snow White and my Pony Pals."

"But you had a good time in Virginia with your godparents and Alicia, didn't you?" Lulu's father said.

"I had an awesome time!" Lulu told him. "Alicia's great. If she lived in Wiggins she would make a perfect Pony Pal. And isn't Jigsaw the cutest pony you ever saw, Dad?"

"An excellent pony," her father agreed.

They pulled into the driveway and got out of the car. Lulu took her suitcase to her room and went back downstairs.

"I'm going out to go see Snow White," she told her father as she ran through the kitchen.

"I have some errands to run," he said. "But I'll be back for dinner."

Lulu headed towards the paddock shouting, "Snow White, I'm home."

When she reached the paddock fence she looked all around the small field for her pony. She couldn't see Snow White anywhere. Snow White's stablemate, Acorn, wasn't there either. Lulu opened the gate and went in. I bet they're both sleeping in the shade behind the shed, thought Lulu.

She went around to the back of the shed. There were no ponies there either. That's when she remembered that she'd asked her Pony Pals, Anna and Pam, to exercise Snow White for her. I bet Pam rode Snow White today, Lulu decided. Anna and Pam are probably on a trail ride with Acorn and Snow White right now.

2

Lulu checked her watch. Four-thirty. She hoped her friends and her pony would be back soon.

Lulu went into the shed. Anna did chores for both their ponies while Lulu was away. Lulu decided to surprise Anna by giving the shed an extra special cleaning.

As she raked the shed, Lulu noticed Snow White's saddle and bridle. I'll clean them too, she thought. Lulu stopped raking and stared at the saddle.

Why was it in the shed? Pam would need it to ride Snow White. She'd never take her on a trail ride bareback.

Had something happened to Snow White? Was she sick?

Lulu went back inside and ran through the house to her grandmother's beauty parlor in the front room.

Grandmother Sanders was cutting a client's dark brown hair. She spoke to Lulu's reflection in the mirror. "Lulu, dear," she said. "I'm so glad you finally came in to see me. Your father was just here."

"I . . . I . . ." began Lulu.

Grandmother turned to her. "Goodness, child," she said, "what's wrong? You look a fright."

"Where's Snow White?" Lulu blurted out. "What's happened to Snow White?"

"Nothing that I know of," Grandmother answered calmly. "Isn't Anna Harley taking care of her?"

Lulu nodded. "Snow White's saddle and everything are in the shed. But she isn't. I thought maybe she got sick or something."

"Not that I've heard," Grandmother said.

Lulu ran out of the shop. "No running in the house, Lucinda," her grandmother called after her. Lulu slowed down—but just a little. This is an emergency, she thought. Grandmother doesn't understand because she doesn't like ponies.

As Lulu came into the kitchen she had an idea. Maybe Anna and Pam had gone trail riding on Acorn and Lightning and left Snow White behind. Lulu remembered that her pony didn't like to be left alone. Twice before she had run away when she was left alone.

4

Has Snow White run away again? Lulu wondered. Or was she sick and at Dr. Crandal's? Panicky thoughts chased one another through Lulu's head. Sick? Lost? Injured? Or dead! What should she do?

Lulu remembered that the first rule in an emergency was to stay calm. She took three slow, deep breaths. When she felt calmer she thought about what to do first.

I'll call Dr. Crandal, she decided, and ask him if Snow White is there. She picked up the kitchen phone and dialed Dr. Crandal's number. His assistant, Henry, answered.

"Could I speak to Dr. Crandal, please?" Lulu asked.

"Dr. Crandal is out on barn calls," Henry answered.

Lulu asked Henry if Snow White was in the animal hospital.

"No," replied Henry.

"Are you sure that Snow White wasn't there at all this week?" asked Lulu.

"Not unless something happened on my day off," he said. "I'll check the computer."

A minute later Henry was back talking on the phone. "Dr. Crandal didn't have an appointment with Snow White this week," he said. "Here *or* at your place."

"She's missing," Lulu said sadly. "She must have run away. Is Pam there?"

"I saw Pam at lunchtime," he answered. "She was riding Lightning towards that trail you kids use."

"Pony Pal Trail," said Lulu.

Pony Pal Trail was a mile-and-a-half trail that connected Pam's place to Snow White's and Acorn's paddock.

"If you see Pam, tell her Snow White's missing," Lulu told Henry.

Henry said he would and wished Lulu good luck. "Snow White's a very special pony," he said.

Tears sprang to Lulu's eyes as she hung up the phone. Snow White *was* a special pony. A special pony that had run away and had an accident before. Lulu was afraid it had happened again. What if this time she couldn't find her pony? What if Snow White was lost and

injured in the woods somewhere—miles from Wiggins?

Lulu took another deep breath. The next thing to do, she decided, was search for Snow White. She'd look for clues on Pony Pal Trail. Maybe she'd meet Anna and Pam and they could all look for Snow White.

Lulu ran upstairs for the supplies she would need for the search. First, she put her binoculars, water bottle, first aid kit, flashlight, a sweater and rain gear in her backpack. Next she changed into her riding boots and put her whistle around her neck.

As Lulu ran down the stairs with her loaded backpack, she reminded herself to pack a halter and lead rope. Those were in the shed.

She decided not to tell her grandmother what she was doing. Her grandmother wouldn't approve and would try to keep her from going.

No one was going to stop her from going into the woods and searching for her pony. Where is Snow White right now? she wondered. What is she doing?

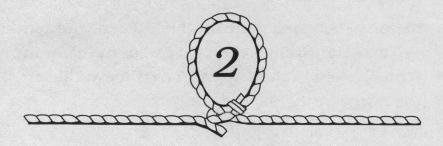

Cards

Lulu decided to leave notes for her father and Anna and Pam. She might need their help. First, she took a package of red ribbon from a kitchen drawer and put it in her backpack. She could tie the ribbon to tree branches to mark her trail.

She wrote a note to her father.

Snow White missing. Went into the woods starting on Pony Pal Trail to look for her. Using red ribbon trail markers.

She folded the paper, sealed it with tape, wrote "Dad" on the outside and put it next to the answering machine on the kitchen counter.

Next, she wrote a note for Anna and Pam in case she didn't meet them. She'd leave that in the shed.

Anna and Pam. Snow White missing. Went into woods starting on Pony Pal Trail. Will leave trail markers of red ribbon on branches. SOS. Please come.

Lulu was halfway across the yard with her backpack when she saw someone coming off Pony Pal Trail. It was Anna! Pam and Lightning were behind her. Great, thought Lulu. We can all go looking for Snow White together.

As Lulu ran towards her friends she felt a little angry. Why did they leave Snow White alone? Didn't they remember the two times that Snow White had already run away?

Suddenly Lulu saw a flash of white coming out of the woods. It was Snow White! A strange boy was riding her. Snow White was safe. She wasn't sick and she hadn't run away.

But who is that boy? wondered Lulu. And why is he riding my pony?

"Lulu! You're back!" shouted Anna. She jumped off Acorn and led him towards Lulu.

Pam rode Lightning over to Lulu. "We thought we'd be back before you got here," she said as she dismounted. "Did you have fun?"

Before Lulu could answer, the stranger galloped Snow White right up to them. You're not supposed to gallop up to people, thought Lulu angrily. It's dangerous. Lulu wondered if the boy was one of Mrs. Crandal's riding students. Why did Pam and her mother let such an irresponsible person ride Snow White?

"Hi," the boy said cheerfully. "You must be Lulu. Snow White's a great pony. She loves western riding."

"Who are you?" Lulu blurted out.

Lulu noticed that the boy was using a big

western riding saddle and bridle on Snow White.

"He's Charlie Chase," Anna said, answering Lulu's question.

"Mr. Olson's nephew," added Pam. "He came the day after you left."

"He lives on a big ranch in Wyoming, but he's at his uncle's horse farm for the whole summer," Anna explained. "Charlie's been exercising Snow White for you. Isn't that great?"

"I thought you and Pam were going to exercise her for me," said Lulu.

Lulu noticed that Snow White was breathing hard and covered in sweat. Charlie had ridden her too hard!

Charlie leant forward over the saddle horn and stroked Snow White's neck. "We've been having fun together, haven't we, Snow White?" he said. Snow White nickered happily as if to agree.

"Didn't you guys ride her at all?" Lulu asked Pam and Anna.

"When Charlie rides with us he uses Snow White instead of his own pony," said Anna. "So we didn't have to."

"My pony's named Moondance," Charlie said as he jumped off Snow White. "He's over at Uncle Reggie's. I ride Moondance all the time." He scratched Snow White's forehead. "But you needed some working out, didn't you, Snow White?"

Lulu couldn't stand how Charlie kept touching Snow White.

"Snow White loves western," Charlie continued. "She took to it right away."

"When I saw her saddle in the shed," Lulu told Anna. "I thought something awful had happened to her."

"Sorry," Anna said. "I didn't think—"

"You should try a western saddle, Lulu," Charlie said, interrupting Anna. "My uncle said you could use this one as long as you want. He agrees with me that Snow White is a perfect western pony. Someone must have ridden her western when she was young."

Lulu hated that Charlie rode Snow White with a big western saddle. And western reining was different from what Snow White was used to. Now her pony would be confused.

"Charlie's a great rider," said Anna.

"I should be good. I rode before I walked," Charlie said. "Anyway, I think you should try western with Snow White, Lulu. I'll show you how."

"I know how," Lulu said. "I prefer English."

Charlie smiled. Or was he laughing at her? She couldn't tell.

"Time to wipe these ponies down, give them some water and put them out in the paddock," Charlie said.

Who does he think he is? wondered Lulu. He's telling everybody what to do as if we don't know how to take care of our own ponies.

"Then we're going to play cards," Anna told Lulu excitedly. "Charlie taught us this neat game all the kids out west play."

Charlie turned Snow White around to take her over to the shed. Lulu grabbed the reins from him, looked him right in the eye and said firmly, "I'll do it."

Charlie didn't let go of the reins. "I rode her so I should do it," he said. "I don't mind."

"I'll do it," Lulu repeated. She couldn't wait to get Snow White away from this creep.

Charlie finally let go of the reins. "Okay," he said cheerfully. "I'll go get us snacks and cards."

"There's some lemonade in the refrigerator," Anna said. "And brownies in the cookie jar."

"Doesn't Anna's mother make the best brownies?" Charlie asked Lulu as he patted Snow White's side again.

Lulu nodded. She was too angry to speak.

Charlie finally left for the house. "Anna," he called over his shoulder, "are the cards still on the kitchen counter?"

"Right where we left them yesterday," Anna shouted after him.

He's acting like he's been Anna's friend all his life, thought Lulu.

"Isn't he great?" Anna said as soon as Charlie was out of earshot.

"He's so much fun," added Pam. "You're going to love this card game."

"I don't think you should have let him ride Snow White western," Lulu told them.

"Snow White liked it," Anna protested. "You could tell."

Lulu lifted off Snow White's saddle and blanket. Her pony's back was dripping wet. "He rode her too hard," Lulu said.

"Not really," Pam told her. "Charlie is an excellent horseman."

"Wait until you see the tricks he does on Moondance," Anna said. "Charlie's showing us how to rope. And we all love to do barrel racing. It's great!"

"In barrel racing you have these three barrels set up like—" Pam began.

"I know what barrel racing is," Lulu interrupted. "I'm going to take Snow White into the shade to wipe her down."

"Meet you at the picnic table," said Pam. She'd already wiped down Lightning.

They didn't even ask me about my trip, Lulu thought as she led Snow White away. All they can talk about is how much fun they had when I was gone.

Lulu loved her Pony Pals. Anna Harley's house was next to Lulu's grandmother's. Acorn and Snow White shared the paddock behind the Harleys' backyard. Anna was fun-loving and full of energy. She was dyslexic so reading and writing were difficult for her. Anna would rather draw than write. She was an excellent artist and loved to draw pictures of ponies.

Pam Crandal, on the other hand, loved to read and write. School was fun for her. But what she loved most was anything to do with ponies and horses. Pam's mother was a riding teacher and her father was a veterinarian, so she had grown up around horses and ponies. Pam had owned a pony for as long as she could remember.

Anna didn't get her own pony until she was nine years old. But she'd taken riding lessons with Pam's mother since she was six. Lulu, too, had ridden lots when she was little, but Snow White was her first pony. Before that she was traveling around too much to have a pony.

Lulu's mother died when she was four years old. Her father traveled all over the world to study and write about wild animals. For many years he took Lulu with him. But when Lulu turned ten her father said she should stay in one place. That's when she moved to Wiggins to live with her grandmother. Lulu didn't like Wiggins, until she met Pam and Anna. Being a Pony Pal made living in Wiggins an adventure.

But now, after her trip to Virginia, her Pony Pals seemed different. It didn't even feel like they were Pony Pals anymore.

Model Ponies

Lulu looked into Snow White's eyes. "I'm back," she said softly. "I'll take care of you now."

She checked her pony's body carefully. There were no nicks or scratches. That was good. She put her head against Snow White's side. Her breathing had calmed down.

"I missed you, Snow White," Lulu said. "I rode another pony, but I wished it was you."

Lulu could see Anna and Pam at the picnic table with Charlie. They were laughing and talking excitedly.

Anna waved to Lulu. "Come on," she yelled. "Snacks are ready."

"And cards!" shouted Pam. "You'll love this game, Lulu."

Charlie put two fingers in his mouth and whistled.

Snow White turned quickly and ran up to the fence near the picnic table.

Lulu didn't call Snow White back to her. She was afraid Snow White wouldn't come. What if Snow White liked Charlie better than her?

I wish I was still in Virginia, thought Lulu as she walked slowly across the paddock.

"Hurry up, Lulu," Pam yelled. "Charlie's dealing the cards."

"I have to unpack," Lulu shouted. "I'll see you later."

"Okay," Charlie said.

As Lulu passed them at the table Pam said, "Come back when you finish. You can play the next game."

"No, thanks," Lulu told her. "I'm pretty tired. I'm going to take a nap. Then I'm having dinner with my father and grandmother. I'll see you tomorrow."

Maybe tomorrow that stupid Charlie won't be around, Lulu thought as she went to her room. She put her suitcase on the bed and opened it to unpack. On top of her clothes she saw an envelope with her name on it. It was Alicia's handwriting. Lulu smiled to herself as she opened the envelope. That's why Alicia closed my suitcase for me, she thought. She wanted to put in this letter.

Lulu sat on the edge of the bed to read it.

Lulu could hear Pam, Anna and Charlie laughing through the opened window. They didn't miss me at all, she thought as she closed the window. She went back to unpacking her suitcase. In the bottom she found a paper bag. She opened the bag and poured out nine plastic ponies. She'd bought them at the horse museum in Virginia. Lulu had looked at hundreds of model ponies in the gift shop. Finally she found three that looked just like Acorn, Lightning and Snow White. She'd bought sets of the three ponies for each of them.

Dear Lulu,

Thank you for coming to visit. I had the BEST time. I hope you will come again soon. The overnight trail ride was the absolute best. I wish you lived in Virginia. Mom and Dad said you should come back whenever you want— even for the whole summer. Mom could come and get Snow White with our horse trailer. She said we always played well together when we were little, too.

Your Pony Pal in Virginia,

Alicia

P S
Don't forget my e-mail address is aliciak@pt.com.

PP S
How's Snow White? How are Pam and Anna? I bet they missed you.

Now she dropped the models back in the brown bag and put the bag in the top drawer of her bureau. She didn't feel like giving Anna and Pam presents anymore.

When Lulu woke the next morning, the first thing she did was look out at the paddock. Snow White and Acorn were grazing side by side in the early morning light. Anna was sitting on the paddock fence drawing a picture of them.

I can't wait to ride Snow White again, thought Lulu. Maybe we can go for a trail ride this morning. Just the Pony Pals.

Lulu dressed, ate a bowl of cereal and ran outside.

When Anna saw her she jumped down from the fence and met her halfway across the yard. "I was hoping you'd get up early," she said.

"Let's call Pam," Lulu said, "and go for a trail ride."

"Pam's coming over," Anna told her. "We can leave as soon as she gets here."

"Great," said Lulu. She called for Snow White. Her pony looked up and trotted over to the gate to meet her.

Lulu opened the gate and threw her arms around Snow White's neck.

"We're going for a trail ride," she told her

pony. "Just the Pony Pals." She turned to Anna. "Where should we go?"

"We're riding over to Olson's farm," Anna answered. "To show you Moondance, and practice roping. Charlie's teaching us how. Lulu, it's so much fun. And Moondance is an amazing pony. Wait until you see him."

"I don't know—" Lulu started to say.

"You have to come," said Anna. "You'll see, western stuff is fun. Charlie is the best rider."

Maybe western stuff *is* fun, thought Lulu. But Charlie isn't. What was wrong with Anna and Pam? Had they turned boy crazy while she was gone?

"I've already fed Snow White," Anna said. "So we can saddle up and be ready when Pam gets here. Are you going to use the western saddle?"

"No!" Lulu practically shouted. "I am not."

Anna looked surprised that Lulu was angry.

"I don't think you should have let Charlie ride her western," Lulu said.

"Sorry," said Anna. "We didn't think you'd mind. I mean . . . he's an excellent rider and—"

"Forget it," Lulu said.

By the time Pam arrived, Snow White and Acorn were saddled up.

Pam was so excited about going to Olson's farm that she didn't even dismount. At least it will be just the three of us riding there, thought Lulu.

Lulu put her foot in the stirrup, pulled herself up and sat in the saddle. She pulled the reins to tell Snow White to turn around. Snow White nickered and threw back her head. It was as if she didn't want to do what Lulu told her anymore.

Charlie Chase ruined my pony, thought Lulu.

Bucket Head

Anna and Pam were already going through the paddock gate towards Main Street. Lulu still didn't have control of Snow White.

"Snow White," she said firmly. "This is English riding. Now pay attention."

Snow White finally calmed down.

Pam led the way up Main Street, onto Belgo Road and past Off-Main Diner. Lulu kept a firm rein on Snow White.

When they reached the entrance to the trail they all stopped.

"Lulu, you can lead the rest of the way," said Pam.

Lulu took the lead. She loved being back on the familiar trail with Snow White and her Pony Pals. She only wished that they weren't on their way to see Charlie Chase.

The girls rode off the trail onto Crosshill Road and towards Olson's Horse Farm. Lulu saw Charlie Chase standing on the lawn near the barn. He was next to a weird-looking model pony. Its body was a wooden barrel. The legs were a saw horse and it had a bucket for the head. As they came closer Lulu noticed that the fake model pony had on a real western saddle and reins.

"That's the pony we sit on to practice roping," Anna said. She giggled. "We call him Bucket Head."

In a corral near the barn Lulu noticed a chestnut pony. When the pony saw the Pony Pal ponies he snorted and ran wildly along the fence line.

"That's Moondance," Pam told Lulu.

"I figured," said Lulu.

"See the half-moon marking on his rump?" asked Anna.

"I see it," answered Lulu. "Do we use the paddock behind the barn?"

"We put our ponies in with Moondance," said Anna as she dismounted.

"Moondance seems a little wild," said Lulu.

Charlie came up to them. "He's just excited to see the other ponies," he told Lulu.

I wasn't talking to you, Lulu thought. But she didn't say it.

Anna had already opened the paddock gate and was leading Acorn inside. Moondance ran over to Acorn and sniffed noses with him.

Pam led Lightning in right behind Anna and Acorn.

Charlie stroked Snow White's cheek. "When you were western riding did you learn any roping?" he asked Lulu.

Lulu ignored his question.

"Have Moondance and Snow White ever been in the same paddock?" she asked.

Charlie thought for a second. "No, but they'll

30

be okay," he answered. "Moondance makes a lot of noise, but he's gentle."

Lulu led Snow White into the corral. The instant Moondance saw her he charged over and tried to bite her on the neck.

"Stop him!" Lulu shouted as she yanked Snow White away.

Pam grabbed Moondance while Lulu led Snow White out of the corral.

"That was a mistake," Charlie said.

"I'll say," said Lulu. "I thought you said he was gentle."

Charlie shook his head and laughed.

"What's so funny?" asked Lulu. "He tried to bite her."

"The mistake," said Charlie, "was taking Snow White out of the corral. You should have left her there. They would have worked it out."

"Are you crazy?" Lulu shouted.

"That's what we do back home," Charlie said. "Snow White and Moondance would be friends by now."

Pam and Anna came up to them.

"Maybe you should put Snow White back in the corral now," Pam suggested.

"Charlie knows a lot about horses," added Anna.

"And I know Snow White," Lulu said firmly. "She doesn't want to be anywhere near a pony that would bite her!" She looked around. The hitching post was empty. "Come on, Snow White," she said as she turned her pony around.

"I'm taking Moondance out of the corral now, anyway," Charlie called after her. "So go ahead and put Snow White in with the other ponies."

Lulu ignored him and kept walking. Anna ran after her. "I'll help you take off Snow White's saddle," she said.

"I'm not taking off her saddle," Lulu told her. "I'm not staying that long."

Lulu tied up Snow White and stroked her forehead. But Snow White watched Moondance and Charlie. "Don't be afraid," Lulu told her. "I'll protect you from that awful pony."

A few minutes later Lulu was standing near the riding ring fence with Anna and Pam. "He'll warm him up first," said Pam.

There were three big metal barrels in the ring.

"He rides Moondance around the barrels in a cloverleaf pattern," Anna explained. "You make a right and two left."

"I know," Lulu said. "I've seen it before. It's not very hard."

"Charlie is really fast," said Pam. She held out a stopwatch. "Do you want to time him?"

"No, thanks," Lulu told her.

Charlie *did* go fast. Moondance tilted so far when he went around the barrels that Charlie's foot touched the ground.

When he'd done the run, he rode over to them.

"You did it in seventeen-point-five seconds," Pam told him. "That's two seconds better than yesterday."

"Good going, Moondance!" Charlie exclaimed. "You should try barrel racing on Snow White, Lulu. She really likes it."

"You did that with Snow White!" Lulu exclaimed. She looked from Anna to Pam. "You let him?"

"He didn't ride her that fast," Anna said.

"You guys are probably sick of watching me," Charlie said. "Let's do some roping."

"First, show Lulu your trick riding," Pam begged.

"Okay," agreed Charlie.

Charlie stood on the front of his saddle with his feet under a special strap that ran behind the saddle horn. Lulu watched in amazement as he stood, arms open, while Moondance walked around the paddock.

"That's so amazing," gushed Anna. "Isn't it, Lulu?"

"It doesn't look safe," commented Lulu.

Charlie dropped back into the saddle and rode over to them. "Now let's rope," he said.

"I'm skipping rope," Lulu told them.

"We're not skipping rope," Charlie joked. "This isn't jump rope."

Anna and Pam laughed and laughed.

Why are they laughing at that lame joke, wondered Lulu? It's the sort of stupid thing Mike Lacey and Tommy Rand would say. Mike and Tommy were the two most obnoxious boys the Pony Pals knew. Lulu thought that Charlie

should hang out with them instead of the Pony Pals.

Lulu watched Pam and Anna take turns sitting on Bucket Head. They tried to twirl a circle of thick rope in the air like a cowboy. Lulu thought they looked silly sitting on Bucket Head.

In between showing them what to do, Charlie showed off his fanciest rope tricks.

Boring, thought Lulu.

"You have to try this," Pam called to Lulu.

Lulu looked at her watch and pretended to be surprised. "It's eleven o'clock!" she exclaimed. "I have to go. I promised my grandmother to help her with . . . uh . . . the garden."

"Too bad," said Charlie. "Catch you later."

Pam and Anna didn't seem to care that she was leaving, either.

Maybe I *will* go back to Virginia, Lulu thought as she walked slowly over to the hitching post. It would be a lot more fun than hanging around with Charlie and his cowgirls.

Tied to a Tree

Lulu was upset the whole trail ride home. How could Pam and Anna think that Charlie Chase was so special? Anybody could see that he was nothing but a show-off.

She took off Snow White's tack and wiped her down. "We don't have to worry about dumb old Charlie and his mean pony anymore," she told Snow White. "We're going to Virginia."

After Lulu put Snow White out in the paddock, she went to the house to talk to her father.

She found him in his room packing for his

trip to Canada. Lulu told him that her godparents and Alicia had invited her back to Virginia.

"They've invited Snow White, too," Lulu added. "They'll drive the horse trailer here and give us a ride."

"You just got home," her father said.

"I know," Lulu said. "But I want to go back. You're not going to be here, anyway."

"Isn't it Alicia's turn to visit you?" he asked.

"I'd rather go to her house," Lulu told him. "We'll have more fun. And I like her friends."

She handed her father a pile of folded T-shirts to pack.

"What about your Pony Pals?" he asked. "Do they know you're leaving again?"

"They won't care," Lulu told him. "Can I call Alicia now and tell her I'm coming?"

"Your godparents did enjoy having you around," Mr. Sanders said. "And they told me they'd love to have you back. But do you really want to go back so soon?"

"I do," said Lulu.

"Do me a favor," he said. "Wait until

tomorrow to decide for sure. You might change your mind."

"Okay," agreed Lulu.

While she helped her father finish packing, he told her about his trip to study black bears— but *she* was thinking about her own trip. As soon as she woke up the next morning she was going to call Alicia. There was no way she was going to change her mind.

Lulu was standing on the sidewalk, waving goodbye to her father, when she saw Pam and Anna riding down Main Street. She was surprised that Charlie wasn't with them.

Lulu went back into the house. From the kitchen window, she saw that Anna and Pam didn't take off Acorn's and Lightning's tack. Instead, they tied them to the fence rail. Lulu wondered what they were going to do next. She didn't have to wait long to find out. Anna and Pam left their ponies and walked towards her house.

Lulu opened the dishwasher and began to empty it. She pretended to be surprised when they came to the screen door.

"Hi," Pam said as she came in.

"You should have stayed yesterday, Lulu," said Anna. "We did barrel racing."

"We came back to invite you to a barn sleepover tonight," said Pam. "It'll be a party to welcome you home."

"Is Charlie coming?" asked Lulu.

Anna giggled. "Of course not," she said. "He's a boy."

"Besides, it's a Pony Pal sleepover," added Pam. "Come on. Tell your grandmother and get your stuff."

"We want to stop at the diner on the way," added Anna.

"Great," said Lulu. "I'm starving."

The Pony Pals all loved Off-Main Diner. Anna's mother owned the diner, so the Pony Pals could eat there whenever they wanted. The only rule was that they had to be their own waiters.

"I'm so glad you're back, Lulu," said Pam.

"We have so much to talk about," said Anna.

"You haven't even told us about your trip," added Pam.

Lulu remembered her presents for Anna and Pam. I'll bring them with me, she thought. I'll tell them about the trip and give them their presents at the diner. Maybe they're finally bored with Charlie and his rope tricks. Maybe we can go back to being Pony Pals. Maybe I won't go back to Virginia.

"We have another surprise for you," Anna said.

"What?" Lulu asked.

"We're having a hoedown," said Pam. "It was Charlie's idea."

"It'll be on Sunday, so we only have a few days to get ready," Anna explained. "Charlie's meeting us at the diner to plan it."

"A hoedown is a western party," added Pam.

"I know what a hoedown is," said Lulu. For the first time she wasn't looking forward to going to the diner.

When the three girls and their ponies reached the diner, Moondance was already at the hitching post.

"I'm tying Snow White to the tree," Lulu told

Pam and Anna. "To keep her away from Moondance."

"You should let Moondance and Snow White work out their problems," Pam said. "After all, they're going to be together for the whole summer."

Oh, no, they're not, thought Lulu. Snow White and Moondance are never going to be friends.

Charlie was already sitting in the Pony Pals' favorite booth. When he saw the three girls come in he went over to meet them.

"I'll take your orders," he said. "I'm having a burger special, root beer and a brownie, of course."

"Same for me," said Anna.

"Me, too," said Pam.

"You, too?" Charlie asked Lulu.

"No," said Lulu. "I'll just have some ginger ale."

"You love the burger special," protested Anna.

"You said you were starving," added Pam.

"I'm not hungry anymore," Lulu told them. "I'll get the drinks."

When Lulu came back to the table with the drinks, Pam was already making a list of events for the hoedown. Anna was working on a poster design. Charlie Chase was running the meeting.

Lulu took the drinks off the tray and put them on the table. She turned to take the tray back to the counter.

"Three Pony Pal Burger Specials on board," the cook called from the kitchen.

"I'm already up," Lulu said over her shoulder. "I'll get them."

Anna jumped up. "I'll help," she said.

"I don't need any help," Lulu told her.

Anna followed Lulu anyway.

"What's wrong?" Anna asked. "Aren't you excited about the hoedown?"

Lulu turned to Anna. "You decided to do a hoedown without even asking me," she angrily whispered. "I thought we had to agree about things like that. And you're treating Charlie like he's a Pony Pal. You're even having a Pony Pal Meeting."

"Charlie isn't a Pony Pal," said Anna. "And this isn't a Pony Pal Meeting."

"It sure feels like one," Lulu told her.

"Well, it's not," said Anna. "It's a hoedown meeting. You should try harder to like Charlie. We need to work together to make the hoedown a success."

I don't have to try harder to do anything, thought Lulu. I'm not even going to your stupid hoedown.

Not a Pony Pal Meeting

Lulu drank her ginger ale and listened to the meeting. She was bored and didn't have many ideas for a hoedown. But Anna and Pam were very enthusiastic and full of ideas.

"Let's do a hay ride," suggested Pam. "Mr. Olson has two Belgian draughthorses. They'd be perfect for that."

"Terrific," said Charlie. "Write it down. I'll set it up with Uncle Reggie."

"I'll ask my father and the other volunteer fire fighters to do the barbecue," put in Anna. "It's a good way for them to make money."

"But let's not charge for anything else," suggested Pam. "Let's just make it a party for fun."

"How are you going to buy prizes for the games?" asked Lulu. "They cost money."

"Good question," said Charlie through a mouthful of half-chewed hamburger.

"My mother has ribbons left over from other horse shows," said Pam. "We can use those."

"Don't forget the costume race," Charlie told Pam. "Put that down."

"You want people to wear costumes?" asked Lulu.

Charlie and Anna exchanged a smile.

"For a costume race you don't wear a costume," Charlie told Lulu. "Putting on the costume is part of the race."

"It's a game," Pam explained. "We put costumes near a pole. Contestants ride up to the pole, jump off their pony, put on the costume and ride back."

"The costumes should be sort of silly," Anna continued, "like a woman's blouse for a boy. It's

47

a surprise for everyone to see what the rider has to put on."

Charlie said that his uncle would play the fiddle for the square dance. One of his uncle's friends would call the square dances.

"A lot of Uncle Reggie's friends want to come," Charlie said. "It's a great chance to show off their roping and barrel racing."

That's because they're show-offs just like you, thought Lulu. She looked at her watch. This meeting was going on forever.

Anna finished the drawings for the poster and Pam added the words. Finally, they had a design that everyone liked.

"The roping games are really fun," Anna told Lulu. "We'll use Bucket Head and a metal bull on wheels."

"I'm going to enter barrel racing," said Pam.

"Me, too," said Anna.

"Are you going to use a western saddle?" asked Lulu.

"No," said Pam.

"We're having a separate barrel race for English riders," Charlie explained. "But you

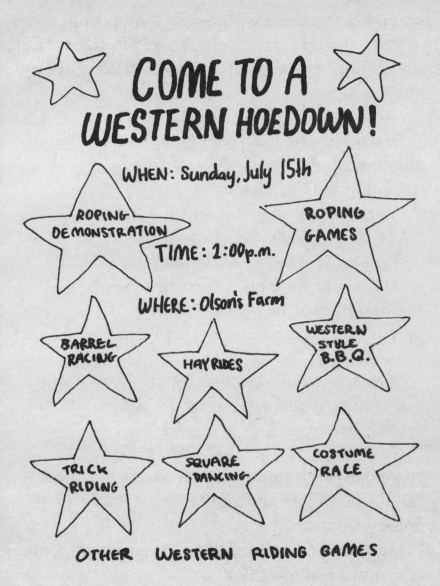

COME TO A WESTERN HOEDOWN!

WHEN: Sunday, July 15th

ROPING DEMONSTRATION

ROPING GAMES

TIME: 2:00p.m.

WHERE: Olson's Farm

BARREL RACING

HAYRIDES

WESTERN STYLE B.B.Q.

TRICK RIDING

SQUARE DANCING

COSTUME RACE

OTHER WESTERN RIDING GAMES

should do western with Snow White, Lulu."

"You should," said Anna and Pam together.

"I'm not going to your hoedown," Lulu blurted out.

"How come?" asked Charlie.

"Because I'm not even going to be here," answered Lulu.

"You're not!" exclaimed Anna.

"Where are you going?" asked Pam.

"Back to Virginia," Lulu told them. "I'm staying for the whole summer."

"But that's so long!" Anna protested.

Charlie leant forward. "I'm going to be here all summer," he said. "So I can exercise Snow White for you."

"No, thank you!" Lulu said sharply. She stood up. "Snow White is coming with me. I'm not leaving her again."

"But, Lulu, you just—" Anna began.

"And I can't come to your sleepover, Pam," Lulu said, interrupting Anna. "I have to go home to pack."

Lulu walked towards the diner door. Pam and Anna ran after her.

"Lulu, wait," called Anna.

"Why are you mad at us?" Pam asked when they caught up with her.

"I told you I was sorry about letting Charlie ride Snow White," whispered Anna. "He's not a Pony Pal and this is not a Pony Pal Meeting."

"I don't understand why you're going back to Virginia so soon," said Pam.

"I just have more fun in Virginia," said Lulu. She pushed through the front door. Anna and Pam didn't follow her.

Lulu ran over to Snow White, put on her helmet, quickly untied Snow White and mounted. Tears stung her eyes.

"I used to have fun in Wiggins," she told Snow White as they turned onto Belgo Road. "Why did it all have to change?"

Two Ideas

Lulu was in her room packing when she heard a loud knock on the kitchen door. She ran downstairs to see who was there.

Pam and Anna were standing at the screen door. When they saw Lulu they opened the door and came in.

"We want to have a Pony Pal Meeting," said Pam. "Right now."

"I'm busy," Lulu told them. "I have to pack for my trip."

"That's what the meeting is about," said Anna. "We don't want you to go away again."

"It's a Pony Pal problem, so the three of us have to talk," explained Pam.

"We've already written down our ideas about why you should stay," added Anna.

"You talked about me in front of Charlie Chase?" Lulu shouted. "I hate that!"

"We did it after he left," said Pam. "Now, let's have our meeting."

"I told you I'm busy," repeated Lulu. "I don't have time for a Pony Pal Meeting."

Pam and Anna exchanged a glance and nodded at one another. They walked past Lulu and started up the stairs.

Lulu went after them. "I didn't say you could stay," she said angrily.

Pam and Anna didn't answer. They walked into Lulu's room.

"I said you have to leave," insisted Lulu.

Pam closed Lulu's half-packed suitcase and put it on the floor. She sat on the edge of the bed. Anna sat on Lulu's desk. Lulu stood in the doorway.

"Leave now," ordered Lulu.

"We're not leaving until you listen to our ideas," said Anna.

"*Then* will you leave me alone?" asked Lulu.

Pam ignored Lulu's question. "Anna, you go first," she said.

Anna opened her backpack and pulled out her drawing pad. She opened to a drawing and held it up. Lulu came over to look at the drawing.

"Acorn is sad because he's all alone," explained Anna. "This is how he'll feel if you take Snow White away."

"Moondance can stay with Acorn," Lulu said.

"Charlie hangs out with you guys all the time anyway."

"It's not the same," explained Anna. "Acorn and Moondance aren't best friends like Acorn and Snow White. Besides, Charlie doesn't live next door."

"Snow White would miss Acorn, too," added Pam.

"Show her your idea, Pam," said Anna. "It's really a good one."

Pam handed Lulu a piece of paper. Lulu silently read it.

Alicia should come and stay with you. Then we could all have fun together.

"Isn't that a great idea?" said Anna.

"Not really," said Lulu.

"Why not?" asked Anna and Pam together.

"Because I want to go back to Alicia's," said Lulu. "I told you, I have more fun there."

"You used to say you had fun in Wiggins," mumbled Anna.

"Didn't you even miss us when you were gone?" asked Pam sadly. "We missed you."

"You did not," said Lulu. "You didn't even care that I came back."

"Well, you didn't act happy to be back," said Pam. "All you did was complain."

"And you didn't even tell us anything about what you did in Virginia that was so much fun," said Anna.

"You were too busy with Charlie and roping and that hoedown," complained Lulu.

"We're not too busy to be Pony Pals," said Anna.

"Then how come all you want to do is hang out with Charlie?" complained Lulu. "We're never just the Pony Pals anymore."

"We're being Pony Pals now," said Pam. "We're having a Pony Pal Meeting."

"Let's go on a trail ride," suggested Anna. "Just the three of us."

"Great idea," said Pam. "Please come, Lulu."

Lulu thought for a minute.

"Okay," she agreed. "But then I have to come home and pack."

The three girls went out to the paddock. While they saddled up their ponies, Lulu told them about her godparents and Alicia. She explained that she and Alicia had been friends when they were really little, before Lulu's mother died. Alicia's mother and Lulu's mother had been friends in college.

"My mother and her mother both loved riding," Lulu explained. "Alicia's family have four horses and two ponies."

The Pony Pals mounted their ponies and rode onto Pony Pal Trail. As they rode, Lulu remembered other things she wanted to tell Pam and Anna.

The girls turned off Pony Pal Trail and rode to their favorite spot on Badd Brook. While the ponies drank water and rested, the Pony Pals skipped stones. Lulu told Pam and Anna about Little Rascal—the pony that she rode.

"He was fast and really cute," she said. "But I missed Snow White."

Next, she told them about the overnight

camping trip with Alicia and two of her friends. "A skunk wandered into our camp site," she said. "I was scared he would spray us. We were all holding our breath."

"Did he spray?" asked Anna.

Lulu shook her head. "We were lucky," she said.

Pam asked Lulu what Alicia was like. "She's just like us," said Lulu. "You'd really like her."

"So let's invite her here," suggested Anna.

"*Please*," begged Pam. "It would be fun to have another rider around. Then Charlie won't be the only one who isn't a Pony Pal."

Lulu watched the three ponies side by side at the edge of the brook. Then she looked around at Anna and Pam. It was great to be a Pony Pal again.

But Lulu still didn't like Charlie and Moondance. And they would be around all summer, too. Should I leave Wiggins to get away from him, she wondered? Or should I invite Alicia to come here?

Would Alicia even want to come to Wiggins?

Dear Alicia

"I don't know if Alicia would want to come." said Lulu. "She has so much fun at home."

"Let's all ask her," suggested Pam. "We could write her a letter together."

"But a letter will take so long in the mail," said Anna. "Alicia will miss the hoedown on Sunday."

"We could phone her," said Pam.

"Or send her an e-mail," suggested Lulu. "She loves to get e-mail."

Pam and Anna both started laughing.

"What's so funny?" asked Lulu.

"You had an idea about inviting Alicia," said Pam. "That means you want her to come here."

"And that you're back to being a Pony Pal," added Anna.

Lulu smiled at her friends.

"Let's go to my place," suggested Pam. "We can write an e-mail to Alicia and have a barn sleepover. Just the three of us." She looked at Lulu. "Okay?"

"Okay," said Lulu. "But if Alicia won't come here, I still might go back to Virginia."

An hour later the three friends were in Mrs. Crandal's barn office. Lulu wrote the first part of the e-mail to Alicia.

Dear Alicia. Hi. I told Pam and Anna about my visit to Virginia and what a great time we had. They want to meet you and Jigsaw. I wondered if you could come here. We could all have so much fun together. I bet your mother would bring Jigsaw for you. There is a boy from Wyoming staying in Wiggins this summer. His name is Charlie Chase. He is a western rider and likes to hang around with us. Pam and Anna like him. I don't. If you don't like him, we'll do our own thing. Please come. Love, Lulu. Next, Anna's going to write.

Hi, I'm Anna. Lulu told us about when the skunk came into your camp site. It must have been exciting and kind of funny. We have lots of adventures when we go camping, too. If you come we will have an overnight trip. I think you will like Charlie. Lulu thinks he's a show-off, but I don't think so. He is lots of fun and a really good rider. We're having this big western party called a hoedown on Sunday. It's going to be lots of fun. I hope you will be here for it. If you come, Jigsaw can stay in the paddock behind my house with Acorn and Snow White. Acorn loves other ponies. So they should get along fine. Hope you can come. That would make us all happy. Bye for now. Anna.

It's Lulu again. Pam is writing next.

I'm Pam Crandal. I'm going to tell you about the

hoedown. We're going to have games, demonstration roping and trick riding. Charlie does all those things. Don't worry if you don't ride western. You can do the games with an English saddle. We have lots of animals at my place, especially horses and ponies. If you come, we'll have sleepover parties in my barn. The Pony Pals do that all the time. I hope you can come. Pam Crandal. PS Send us an e-mail with your answer.

After the Pony Pals sent the e-mail to Alicia, they went to Pam's house and made a picnic supper. They ate it on a large flat rock next to the big paddock.

When they finished eating, Pam and Anna taught Lulu the new card game. Lulu liked the game, especially when she won. While they played she forgot all about Virginia and Charlie Chase and being angry at her friends. She even forgot about Alicia.

It was Pam who remembered. "Let's go in and check the e-mail," she suggested. "And see if Alicia has answered us."

The three friends ran to the barn. Pam went

on-line and checked for messages. There was a message from Alicia. Pam opened the message and read it out loud.

Hi, Pony Pals! Guess what? I talked to my mother and I can come on Saturday for two weeks. Mom will trailer Jigsaw, so I'll have my pony. I'm going to miss my friends, but I still want to come. We call ourselves the Pony Pals, too. We got the idea from you. Is that okay? I can't wait to see Wiggins and meet Pam and Anna. I love meeting new people! Charlie sounds neat. I think western riding is great. So does Jigsaw. I'm bringing my English and western saddles with me. See you on Saturday. I'm so excited. Lulu, did Pam and Anna like their presents? Alicia.

The Pony Pals turned to one another, hit high fives and shouted, "All-right!"

"What presents?" Anna asked Lulu.

Lulu smiled at Pam and Anna. "They're in my backpack," she said.

Lulu went over to her backpack and dug

through it. The bag from the horse museum was on the bottom. She pulled it out and threw it to Pam.

"I bought myself a present, too," Lulu said. "They're all in there."

Pam opened the bag and reached in. She pulled out a model pony that looked just like Acorn.

"Oh-h!" exclaimed Anna as she took the model from Pam. "It's perfect."

Pam dug into the bag again. This time she pulled out two models—one that looked like Snow White and another one that looked like Acorn.

"Lightning is in there somewhere," Lulu told Pam. "Just pour them out."

Pam emptied the bag onto her mother's desk.

"There's a set of three ponies for each of us," Lulu explained.

Anna lined up her three model ponies on the desk. Then she gave Lulu a kiss on the cheek. "Thank you," she said.

Pam thanked her, too.

"I didn't want to give them to you in front of Charlie," Lulu explained.

"I'm glad you didn't," said Pam. "Now is the perfect time. When we all feel like Pony Pals again."

"Uh-oh!" exclaimed Anna. "We forgot to make the posters for the hoedown. If we don't have posters no one will know about it. No one will come."

"Let's do it now," suggested Lulu.

"And we'll put them up first thing tomorrow," said Pam.

The three friends went to Pam's house to get art supplies. They made the posters at the big round table in the Crandals' kitchen.

After they'd made six posters, they brought their sleeping bags up to the hay loft.

The Pony Pals lay in the dark talking about Alicia's visit and the hoedown.

Maybe the hoedown will be fun after all, thought Lulu. But I'm never going to like Charlie Chase.

The Vote

The next morning the Pony Pals put a poster in the barn for Mrs. Crandal's students. Next, they rode to town and put posters in the diner, the feed store and the Green Market.

Lulu and Pam stayed with the ponies, while Anna ran into the library with a poster.

"That leaves one poster for Olson's Horse Farm," Pam told Lulu. "We'll go there next. Are you going to practice barrel racing with us today?"

"I'm not going with you to Olson's," Lulu said. "I have to get ready for Alicia."

"Can you help us find clothes this afternoon to use for the costume race?" asked Pam.

"If you come back here," Lulu answered. "We can look in my grandmother's attic. There're loads of old clothes up there."

The rest of the morning Lulu cleaned her room and shopped for groceries. After lunch Anna and Pam came over. Lulu was glad that Charlie wasn't with them.

The three girls had great fun going through the old clothes in Grandmother Sanders' attic. They laughed hardest when Anna put a strapless red gown over her jeans and T-shirt. The T-shirt had a picture of a horse on it and the horse's head was looking out over the top of the gown.

The next day was Saturday. Anna and Lulu met in the paddock after breakfast.

"Please come over to Olson's farm with us this morning," begged Anna. "We're having so much fun getting ready for the hoedown."

Lulu couldn't imagine having fun with Charlie Chase. "I'm going to make a special lunch for Alicia and her mother," Lulu told

Anna. "Then Alicia and I are going to ride. I want to show her some of our favorite trails."

"We'll come back and ride with you," said Anna. "I'm dying to meet Alicia."

"Will Charlie come?" asked Lulu.

Anna shook her head. "He's practicing riding tricks this afternoon," said Anna. "We were going to watch, but we'll ride with you and Alicia instead."

"Great!" said Lulu.

Lulu made a green salad, baked beans, ham sandwiches, lemonade and chocolate chip cookies for lunch. She was taking the last batch of cookies out of the oven when she heard a car and trailer pull into the driveway.

She ran outside waving and calling, "Yeah! You're here."

Alicia ran towards Lulu. The two friends met and hugged.

"This is so exciting!" exclaimed Alicia. "I can't believe I'm here."

"Me, either," shouted Lulu. "This is so great!"

"Is anyone going to help me get this poor pony out of the trailer," called Alicia's mother.

Snow White whinnied as if to say, "Hey, what's going on?"

"Your new friend, Jigsaw, is here," called Lulu.

Alicia's mother went inside to say hello to Grandmother Sanders, while Lulu and Alicia took care of Jigsaw.

The girls led the gray-and-white pony out of the horse trailer towards the paddock. Snow White stood at the fence watching suspiciously.

"I hope they like one another," said Alicia.

"We should introduce them slowly," suggested Lulu.

When Jigsaw reached the gate Snow White whipped around and charged along the fence line.

"She usually likes new ponies," Lulu told Alicia.

Lulu went into the paddock and called Snow White's name. Snow White slowed down and finally stopped.

Lulu talked soothingly to her pony.

Jigsaw nickered softly, as if to say, "Let's be friends."

Snow White turned and walked over to him.

When Snow White was closer Jigsaw nickered again. This time Snow White answered with a friendly nicker. Alicia and Lulu smiled at one another. Their ponies were going to be friends.

Grandmother Sanders came out with Alicia's mother. Lulu and Alicia served lunch in the backyard. Everyone said it was delicious. After lunch Alicia's mother left for her long drive back to Virginia and Lulu's grandmother went back to work.

After they cleaned up from lunch, Lulu and Alicia waited on the paddock fence for Anna and Pam. Lulu couldn't wait to introduce Alicia to her Pony Pals. But she was nervous, too. What if they didn't like one another the way she didn't like Charlie?

Lulu had nothing to worry about. Pam and Anna liked Alicia right away.

"Jigsaw is just as cute as Lulu said he was," Anna told Alicia.

"So is Acorn," said Alicia. "And Lightning is so pretty. Lulu said she is a great jumper."

"She's great at barrel racing, too," Pam told Alicia.

"I love barrel racing!" exclaimed Alicia. "I brought my western saddle and everything."

"We're doing it with English," Anna said.

"Are you doing it English or western?" Alicia asked Lulu.

Lulu shook her head. "Neither," she answered. "Come on, let's stop gabbing and go for a trail ride."

"Are we going to the horse farm?" asked Alicia. "Am I going to meet Charlie next?"

"He's busy this afternoon," said Lulu.

"He's practicing his trick riding," Pam told her.

"I'd love to watch that," Alicia said.

"Pam and Anna were there all morning," Lulu told Alicia.

"I don't mind going back," said Anna. "I love to watch the trick riding."

"Me, too," said Pam. "Then we can practice barrel racing one more time before the hoedown."

I'm the only one who doesn't want to go to

Olson's farm, thought Lulu. It's three against one.

"So let's ride there," she said.

An hour later the four girls were watching Charlie Chase ride around the ring standing on Moondance's back.

"Charlie is amazing," Alicia told Lulu. "He's so in tune with his pony."

Next, Mr. Olson and Charlie were practicing roping a real calf. "They're doing break away roping," Alicia told the Pony Pals.

"What's that?" asked Anna.

"They use a special rope," explained Alicia. "The calf can break free as soon as it's caught. It's nicer for the calves."

When they finished Charlie walked Moondance over to them.

"That was great," Alicia told Charlie. "Thanks."

Soon everyone but Lulu was barrel racing. She went over to Snow White. They'd put her and Jigsaw together in the small paddock. But Jigsaw was barrel racing now, so Snow White was alone. Lulu went into the paddock and lay her head against Snow White's side. "I'm the only one who isn't having a good time," she told her pony.

But Snow White wasn't listening. She was watching the other ponies racing around the barrels.

Hoedown

Alicia and the Pony Pals spent Sunday morning at Olson's. There were a lot of last minute things to do for the hoedown. At one o'clock they gave their ponies a special grooming, then they changed into jeans and western style shirts. Mr. Olson gave the girls cowboy hats.

"Now you look perfect for a hoedown," he said.

Pam was in charge of showing people where to park. Alicia, Anna and Lulu welcomed them when they came over to the riding ring. Mr.

Olson and the two other musicians played lively country music on a stage near the riding ring.

Lulu was surprised at how much she enjoyed watching the western games. The first event was barrel racing. Pam won first place in junior division barrel racing—English style—and Anna won second. All their practice had paid off. Ms. Wiggins, a friend of the Pony Pals, won first prize in the adult division and Pam's mother won second prize.

Next was junior division barrel racing for western riders. Charlie didn't ride in that race. He was so good that his uncle told him to race with the adults.

Alicia and Jigsaw were even faster than they had been the day before. Alicia was racing against kids who rode western all the time, but she still won the third place ribbon.

Charlie and Moondance won second prize in the adult division. Mr. Olson and his horse, Handsome, took the first place prize.

The other games were fun, too. Lulu and Snow White entered the costume race. The crowd roared with laughter when she galloped to the finish line with a woman's polka dot bikini over her jeans and western shirt. But the biggest laugh was for Charlie. He had to put a lace blouse over his shirt and a woman's long blonde wig under his helmet. He was laughing, too, as he re-mounted Moondance.

"Charlie is a good sport," Alicia observed. "I know a lot of guys who would not have put those on."

"Tommy Rand or Mike Lacey would never do something like that," said Anna.

Lulu took out her camera and clicked a photo of Charlie crossing the finish line. He grinned at Lulu. She smiled back.

After lunch they had the roping demonstration. Everyone applauded when a live calf came into the ring.

Lulu was thinking that Charlie really was a great roper when Moondance stumbled. Charlie Chase fell to the ground with a thump.

A gasp rose from the crowd. But before anyone could be too worried, Charlie and Moondance were back on their feet. Charlie took off his helmet and led his pony out of the ring.

"Let's go," said Pam.

The Pony Pals and Alicia ran over to Charlie to be sure he and Moondance were okay.

"What happened?" Alicia asked.

"Are you okay?" asked Anna.

"Moondance is favoring his back right leg," observed Pam.

Charlie brushed the dirt off his face with the back of his hand. He held up a horseshoe with the other hand. "He threw a shoe," Charlie told them. "I don't think he's hurt."

"But you shouldn't ride him again until it's fixed," a man's voice said.

Lulu turned to see Dr. Crandal.

"Let's be sure he didn't strain anything," Dr. Crandal said as he gently felt Moondance's back right leg. When he finished he smiled up at Charlie. "It seems okay."

"What about your trick riding?" Pam asked Charlie.

"I guess we'll have to skip it," Charlie said.

"But that's the best event," said Alicia sadly. "Can't you ride another pony?"

"I've only done that stuff on Moondance and—" Charlie didn't finish the sentence. He looked at Lulu.

"Did you do those tricks with Snow White?" asked Lulu.

"She was perfectly safe," said Pam.

"We didn't tell you because you were so crabby about Charlie riding her," put in Anna.

"Snow White let you do those tricks!" exclaimed Alicia.

"Charlie has a way with ponies," commented Pam.

"And Snow White is a special pony," said Charlie.

Lulu was speechless. She never imagined that Snow White would gallop with a rider standing on her back. She felt proud of her pony.

"You're furious at me, right?" Charlie asked Lulu.

Lulu shook her head. "You can ride her for the tricks," she said.

People applauded. Lulu looked around and saw that a small crowd had gathered around them.

Lulu helped Charlie change Snow White into the western tack. Snow White nickered happily when Charlie mounted her. Lulu felt only a little jealous.

She checked the cinch one last time. "Be careful," she told Charlie.

Mr. Olson rode Handsome into the ring ahead of Charlie and Snow White. The two riders galloped around the ring.

"Is Mr. Olson doing tricks, too?" Lulu asked Pam.

Pam shook her head. "Handsome is the lead horse. The lead horse rides ahead of the trick horse to keep her steady."

Charlie was riding without reins and smiling at the crowd. "Charlie will start with a single vault," the announcer said.

Suddenly Charlie threw his right leg over the saddle horn and jumped to the ground. His feet landed in front of Snow White's left shoulder. In an instant he was back in the saddle. Snow White kept moving at an even gallop throughout the trick.

The crowd cheered. And so did Lulu.

Next, Charlie did a double vault. First he jumped off Snow White to the right, then to the left. The crowd went wild.

"And now, folks, we have a hippodrome stand," the announcer said.

Lulu held her breath as Charlie squatted on top of Snow White and slipped his feet in a strap behind the saddle horn.

"Don't worry, Lulu," Pam said. "Charlie said Snow White has the steadiest canter of any pony he's ever ridden."

"That's what makes her perfect for this trick," added Anna.

Handsome and Snow White began to gallop. Charlie stood on Snow White's back. He put his hands up in front of him as he rode around the ring. Lulu clicked a photo.

The crowd didn't applaud until Charlie was safely seated in the saddle again. Then they went crazy.

"Snow White was wonderful!" exclaimed Alicia.

Lulu turned and smiled at her. "She was," she said. "And Charlie was pretty amazing, too."

"We're going to have so much fun this week," Alicia said.

Lulu looked at Charlie coming out of the ring with Snow White, then at her Pony Pals and Alicia beside her. Alicia is right, she thought. We *are* going to have fun. She couldn't wait to ride Snow White western.

Lulu ran over to Snow White and Charlie. Charlie dismounted and handed her the reins.

"Thanks for lending me your pony," he said.

"You're welcome," Lulu said. "You were both great."

Snow White nuzzled against Lulu's shoulders. Lulu patted her cheek. "You were great too, Snow White," she said softly. "I love you."

Dear Reader:

I am having a lot of fun researching and writing books about the Pony Pals. I've met many interesting kids and adults who love ponies. And I've visited some wonderful ponies at homes, farms, and riding schools.

Before writing Pony Pals I wrote fourteen novels for children and young adults. Four of these were honored by Children's Choice Awards.

I live in Sharon, Connecticut, with my husband, Lee, and our dog, Willie. Our daughter is all grown up and has her own apartment in New York City.

Besides writing novels I like to draw, paint, garden, and swim. I didn't have a pony when I was growing up, but I have always loved them and dreamt about riding. Now I take riding lessons on a horse named Saz.

I like reading and writing about ponies as much as I do riding. Which proves to me that you don't have to ride a pony to love them. And you certainly don't need a pony to be a Pony Pal.

Happy Reading,

Jeanne Betancourt